Get Dad

Series created by **Roderick Hunt** and **Alex Brychta**

Written by Roderick Hunt
Illustrated by Alex Brychta

BEFORE READING
Talk together
- Look at the picture and talk about what Dad is doing.
- Read the title together and guess why the story is called *Get Dad*.
- Look through the book and talk about the pictures.

About the words in this book
- Your child should be able to sound out and blend some words, which may include:

get   Dad   Mum   on   Biff

- Some words may be more challenging. Encourage or model blending, then read the words below to your child if necessary.

go   Chip   Kipper

DURING READING
Enjoy the story together. If your child needs support to read the words:

- Ask your child to point from left to right under each word whilst reading.
- Model how to sound out and blend new words if necessary.
- If a word is still too tricky, simply say the whole word for your child.
- Use the pictures to talk about the story and learn the meaning of new words.

See the inside back cover for more ideas.

Go on, Dad!

Get Biff.

Go on, Dad!

Get Chip.

Go on, Dad!

Get Kipper.

Go on, Mum!

Get Dad.